Maria's Marvelous Bones

Written by Dr. Carrie Kollias

Illustrations by Gill Guile

Tellwell Talent
www.tellwell.ca

ISBN
978-0-2288-0221-1 (Hardcover)
978-0-2288-0222-8 (Paperback)
978-0-2288-0220-4 (E-Book)

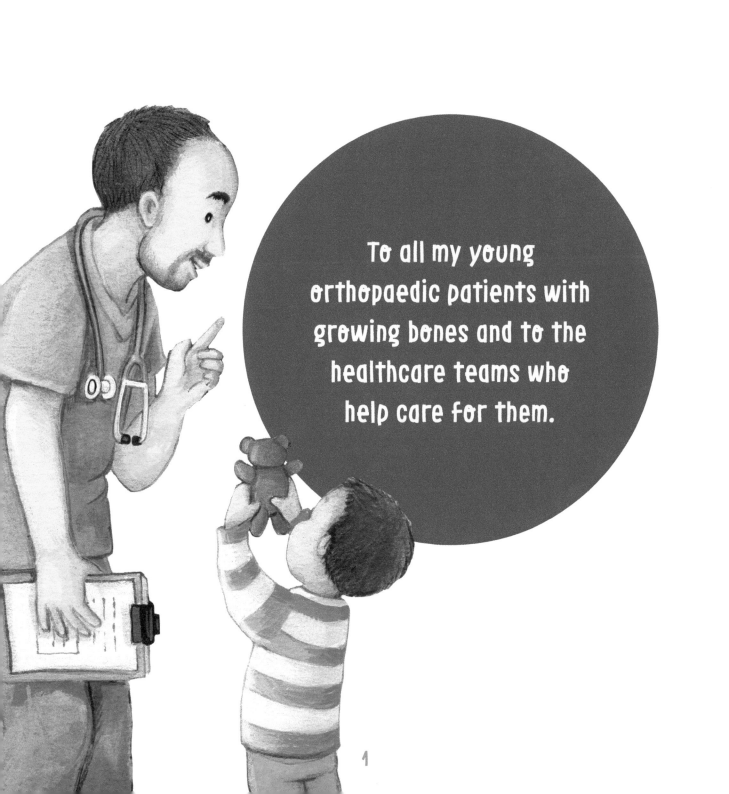

To all my young orthopaedic patients with growing bones and to the healthcare teams who help care for them.

1

This is MARIA.
She likes drawing
pictures.

She also likes
RUNNING,

and
CLIMBING
TREES.

4

Maria has a little brother. His name is TASO.
She loves him a lot, but sometimes he tries to take her
green markers!

One day, Maria and Taso were feeling bored. For fun, they decided to take turns jumping off the couch.

It was Taso's turn.

Maria sat on the top of the couch to watch. She was laughing very hard at Taso. Suddenly, she FELL OFF backwards...

OwWwWIeEee!!!

Maria started to cry. Her arm looked strange, and it HURT.

Taso yelled, "Mommeee—Mommeee—Mommeee help!!!!!!!!" Mommy was at work, but Daddy came running. He looked at Maria's arm and gently placed it on a pillow.

Off they went to the hospital.

At the hospital, they went to the Emergency Department. They saw LOTS of people waiting in chairs.

Maria and her Daddy talked to a friendly nurse named Peter. Maria told Peter the story of how she hurt her arm.

Maria wanted to cry big loud tears, but she tried to be BRAVE.

Peter, the nurse, asked Maria how much her arm hurt. He also asked her to move her fingers.

Then, he wrapped a band around Maria's arm. He called it a "blood pressure cuff". It felt tight, but just for a few moments.

Peter said it was checking how well Maria's HEART was working to pump blood around her body.

Next, he put a special CLIP on Maria's finger. The clip made a beeping sound. He said it was an oxygen monitor to make sure she was breathing okay.

Maria thought it looked like a finger PUPPET!

Another nurse came. She smiled at Maria and asked her to lie down on a special bed, called a "stretcher".

The nurse said they needed to start an IV LINE in Maria's arm. It would give Maria some medicine to feel better.

The nurse cleaned a spot on Maria's arm. Then, Maria felt a tiny little pinch and the nurse started the IV. Maria started feeling BETTER, very quickly.

After the IV was started, Maria met Dr. Mark. Dr. Mark was the emergency room doctor. Maria wiggled her fingers for him, too.

Then, Dr. Mark looked at Maria's arm. He said the nurse would give Maria more medicine. This medicine would make Maria go to sleep.

The doctor said they would take an X—RAY of Maria's arm when she was sleeping. He explained that an x-ray is a picture of bones. The picture is taken with a special camera that can see through skin.

Dr. Mark said he would also make Maria's arm straight when she was sleeping. Maria would not feel her arm hurt, and she would not remember anything.

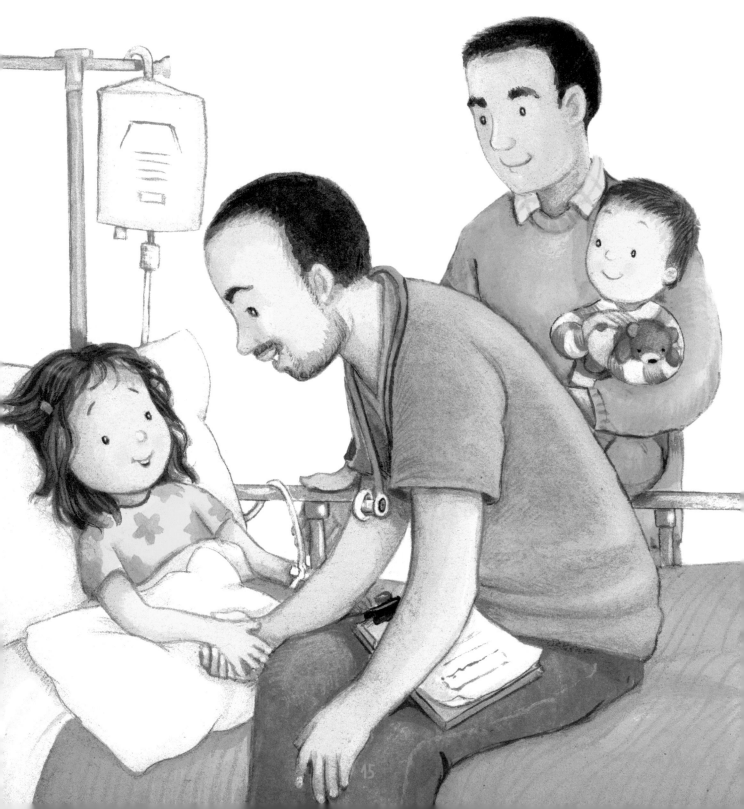

Suddenly, Maria woke up from a very nice dream.

Dr. Mark said, "Great job, Maria! Thanks for being so brave today."

She looked down at her arm. There was a cast on it.
The cast was
GREEN!

Her arm looked straight, and it felt much better.

Dr. Mark sent Maria for another x-ray. This time Maria was awake. The x-ray lady gave her a special x-ray suit to wear over her clothes.

Maria was curious to see what her bones looked like.

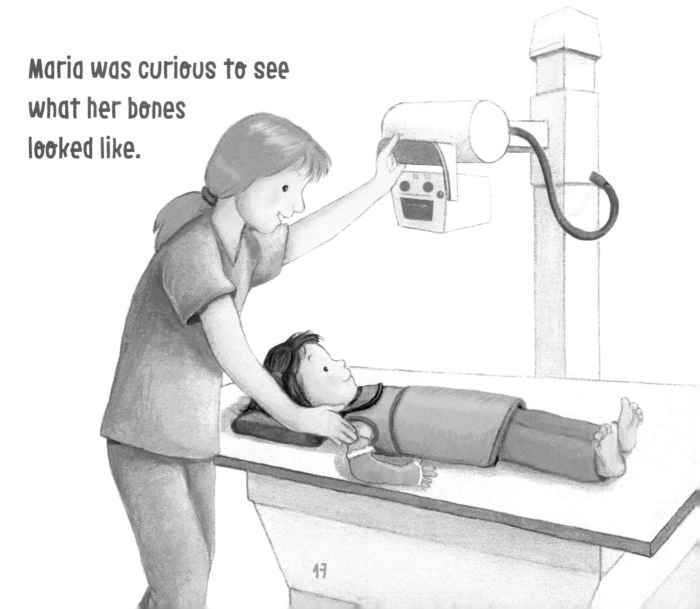

Dr. Mark showed the X-RAYS to Maria and her family. Mommy was there now, too.

They saw pictures of Maria's arm when it was crooked and another picture after it was straightened.

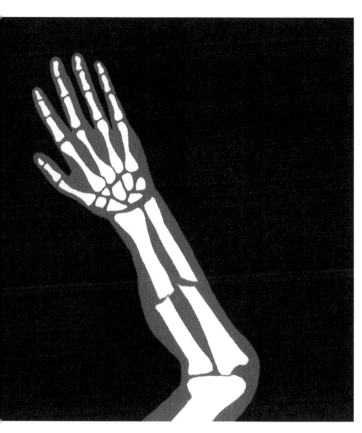

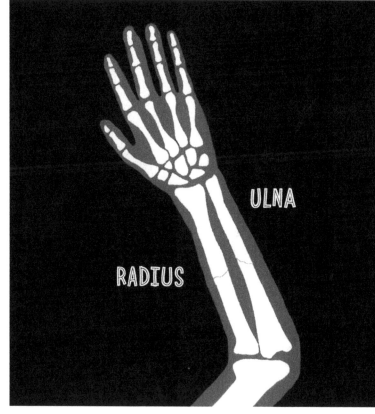

Dr. Mark told Maria,
one bone was called the
"RADIUS" , and the other
bone was called the **"ULNA"**.

Dr. Mark also said another word for a broken bone
was a "fracture".

Two weeks went by. It was time for Maria to go back to the hospital for a checkup.

Maria had x-rays taken again. Then, she met Dr. Anna—the bone doctor. Dr. Anna was the kind of doctor who fixes people's broken arms or legs.

Dr. Anna said, "Your x-rays look good, but that cast is looking a bit STINKY. Would you like us to change it?"

Maria had tried hard to take care of her cast, but she had accidentally spilled milk and spaghetti sauce on it.

Dr. Anna said
Maria's body was making

"CALLUS".

She explained that "callus" was
a big ball of bone glue. The glue
had calcium in it, to make the
broken bones heal.

Next, Maria met Marsha. Marsha was an expert at making casts. She was going to take the stinky cast off, using a tool, called a cast remover.

The cast remover would make a BUZZING noise and the cast would get a little warm, but Maria would be just fine.

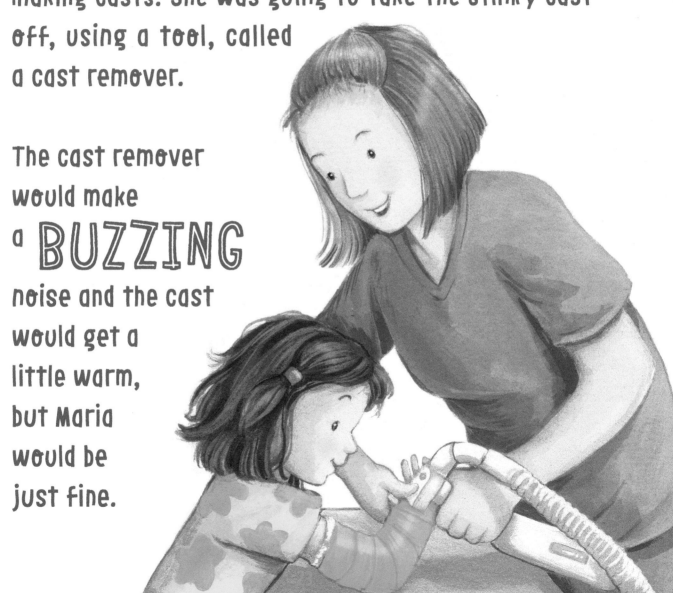

Just like Marsha promised, the stinky cast came off. Marsha asked what color Maria wanted for her new cast. **"GREEN OF COURSE!"** said Maria.

Marsha cleaned Maria's arm and made a new cast for her.

24

Four weeks later, Maria came back for her final x-ray.

Dr. Anna looked at the x-ray and said, "Good job healing your bones. Look at all that new bone! Time for the cast to come off. You don't need it anymore!"

When the cast came off, Maria's arm felt good, but her elbow didn't move that well yet. Dr. Anna said it would move properly in a few weeks. She told Maria swimming would **HELP.**

"Stay safe,
Maria,"
said Dr. Anna.
"Eat lots of
vegetables
to keep your
bones
strong!"

Maria giggled.
That sounded
like a
GOOD
PLAN.

Maria and Taso walked out of the hospital together.

They were ready for a new adventure.

Maria's marvelous
BONES ARE STRONG!

About the Author

Dr. Carrie Kollias is a Canadian orthopaedic surgeon who specializes in the care of children. She has a very helpful husband and two young kids who listen to a lot of stories about bones.

About the Illustrator

Gill Guile loves painting and has illustrated over 600 children's books. She enjoys spending time with her family and playing lots of tennis.

CPSIA information can be obtained
at www.ICGtesting.com
Printed in the USA
LVHW021515290819
629404LV00019B/318/P